Twilight, Say Cheese!

Also by Daisy Sunshine

Sapphire's Special Power

UNICORN University

#1

Twilight, Say Cheese!

by DAISY SUNSHINE
illustrated by MONIQUE DONG

ALADDIN
New York London Toronto Sydney New Delhi

ALADDIN
An imprint of Simon & Schuster Children's Publishing Division
1230 Avenue of the Americas, New York, New York 10020
First Aladdin paperback edition February 2021

Also available in an Aladdin hardcover edition.

Book designed by Laura Lyn DiSiena
The illustrations for this book were rendered digitally.
The text of this book was set in Tinos.
Manufactured in the United States of America 0121 OFF
2 4 6 8 10 9 7 5 3 1
Library of Congress Cataloging-in-Publication Data
Names: Sunshine, Daisy, author.
Title: Twilight, say cheese! / by Daisy Sunshine ; illustrated by Monique Dong.
Description: First Aladdin paperback edition. | New York : Aladdin, 2021. | Series: Unicorn U ; [1] | Audience: Ages 6 to 9. | Summary: A shy unicorn who magically becomes invisible when nervous tries to navigate her first day at boarding school.
Identifiers: LCCN 2019056182 (print) | LCCN 2019056183 (ebook) |
ISBN 9781534461659 (paperback) | ISBN 9781534461666 (hardcover) | ISBN 9781534461673 (ebook)
Subjects: CYAC: Unicorns—Fiction. | First day of school—Fiction. |
Boarding schools—Fiction. | Schools—Fiction. | Anxiety—Fiction.
Classification: LCC PZ7.1.S867 Tw 2021 (print) | LCC PZ7.1.S867 (ebook) | DDC [Fic]—dc23
LC record available at https://lccn.loc.gov/2019056182
LC ebook record available at https://lccn.loc.gov/2019056183

For lovers of sparkles, rainbows, and magic

CONTENTS

1

Ruby-Red Barns

Twilight was having an almost perfect day. The sun was shining, and the yellow buttercups of Sunshine Springs were in full bloom. Her mother had even surprised her with her very favorite breakfast, apple oat muffins with cinnamon sugar. It was a long trip from their farm to Unicorn University, but Twilight's father made it a great adventure and told funny stories and ideas the whole way.

The day was only *almost* perfect because Twilight could not stop thinking about how nervous she was to start school. She worried that she wouldn't know the right things to say or do. Outside her family, she had never spent much time with other unicorns. Her sister Sunset was outgoing, and her sister Dusk was funny. But Twilight had always been shy. How was she going to make friends?

"Look, Twilight! There's Unicorn U!"

Twilight looked up to where her mother's golden horn was pointing. She could see a cluster of big ruby-red barns standing atop the grassy hill in the distance.

Twilight felt her stomach drop. Her nervousness might have just been in the back of her mind on the way there, but now the situation felt very, very real. She felt positively sick.

Twilight thought about telling her parents that she was actually too sick to go to school, but she had decided to make her family proud, swallow her fears, and go. Even if it did make her stomach flip and flop.

"Sugarplum for your thoughts?" Twilight's father asked. He nudged her cheek with his long, gray nose.

"Same old thing, I guess. I'm worried about starting school," Twilight told him.

Twilight's father neighed knowingly. "Of course you are, honey. Everyone is, on their first day, and your sisters were too. But Sunset and Dusk did wonderfully at Unicorn U. You are sure to follow in their hoofprints."

Twilight nodded, though his words didn't actually make her feel any better. When Sunset had been at Unicorn U, she'd been the star of the school hoofball team. Her magical ability let her fly with just a run and a jump, and now she worked with dragons in Cloud Kingdom. Dusk had had the best grades in school and could make flowers grow just by breathing on them. Since graduating, she'd been developing a brand-new apple tree that could grow in any of the five kingdoms.

It was a lot to live up to.

Unlike her sisters, Twilight didn't like to stand out from the crowd. She preferred quiet activities, like reading and painting. Painting was the perfect way to record all her wild daydreams, and books had all the company she could need.

When Twilight had been little, she'd loved reading about magical creatures, especially lions and mice. Lions reminded her of her sisters—always stomping in after practice or conducting experiments. Mice reminded her of herself—quiet and observant. Twilight never minded being the quiet one. She liked watching the goings-on of her house from her favorite spot by the window. It just felt like her role in the family.

That was, until her magical ability had appeared.

She'd discovered it when Dusk had come home one afternoon and jumped from behind a haystack while Twilight had been out in the field, painting and lost in thought. Twilight didn't even realize she had become invisible until Dusk started panicking and yelling for her. Twilight quickly appeared again, just in time to comfort her sister.

Ever since that day, Twilight's invisibility had come and gone unexpectedly. She usually became invisible when she was embarrassed or nervous, but she would always reappear again once her family noticed that she had disappeared, which usually meant she had to whinny or stomp to get their attention. Her parents called her invisibility a magical gift, but Twilight thought of it as a curse. Having to make a spectacle to get a unicorn's attention? That was decidedly too lionlike.

What if I fade out in front of everyone at school? Twilight worried, shuddering at the thought. The last thing she wanted was to be forced to make a scene in front of her classmates.

Twilight's mother trotted over, her well-worn leather satchel swinging gently from her neck. She carried a large pink tulip in her mouth. Carefully she tucked the flower behind Twilight's ear. "You just be yourself, honey," she said.

Twilight let out a soft thank-you neigh, and this time she did feel a little better. She looked down at the ground, and smiled at how her bright purple hooves stood out against her jet-black coat. Dusk had given her a hooficure the night before, to celebrate her first day of school. At first Twilight had worried that it was too flashy, but Dusk convinced her that everyone would have hooficures and that this would help her fit in.

Twilight looked back up at her mom and dad, whose loving smiles gave her a small boost of confidence. Twilight didn't know if she was ready for Unicorn University, but she wanted to try. She stood up straight and smiled back at them.

"Look out, world!" her father neighed merrily. "Twilight is going to school!"

2

Disappearing Act

"I am not going to school," Twilight told her parents. But they were too distracted by the school's impressive grounds to notice.

The three of them had just arrived at the Unicorn University Welcome Picnic on the school's main lawn. This was called the Looping Lawn. It was a large grass-covered hill that connected the Silver Lining Stables, the Crystal Library, and the Wondering Woods.

The Silver Lining Stables, which weren't actually silver but were more like big red barns, were where students would live during the year. Large sliding doors with bright white borders stood open, as if welcoming students inside.

Flower boxes bursting with plants of every color decorated the windows. And a weather vane perched on top of each building. The large metal structures all spun slowly with the wind's changing directions.

"Your stable has the sailboat weather vane on top," Twilight's mother said.

"Same one as Dusk," her fathered remembered. "Sunset was in the stable with the cloud weather vane, which was rather fitting."

Twilight smiled. It was comforting to think of her sisters in this strange new place.

"And that's the library!" her father cheered, motioning toward the building on the other side of the lawn. The castle-like structure sparkled in the distance.

The school was so big and important-looking. It made Twilight feel as if pixies were dancing jigs her in stomach. But her parents were so proud of her, and she didn't want to ruin it by telling them how worried she was. She tried to put on a happy face.

"It looks as if it's really made of crystal," Twilight said.

Her mother laughed softly. “That’s because it is!”

Twilight could only stare in wonder. Her sisters had told her about the library, but they tended to exaggerate. Neither of them could resist a good story, and Twilight had learned to take most things they said with a dash of salt. This time it seemed that they hadn’t explained enough.

“Come on, you two! There’s a party happening!” Twilight’s father called over his shoulder as he trotted toward the welcome picnic.

“He’s right! Let’s go join the fun,” Twilight’s mother said. She galloped after Twilight’s father.

Twilight shook her head. Her parents were outgoing and carefree, and very different from Twilight. At home that felt right. Twilight took care of the little things, and she felt like she was an important part of the family. But here at Unicorn University, with its bright colors and large buildings? It seemed as if she needed a much bigger personality in order to belong. Reluctant and timid, Twilight slowly followed her partying parents.

The center of the Looping Lawn was filled with unicorn

fillies and colts laughing, prancing, and calling out to each other. Sugarplums and candied apples were piled high on a snack table, and a rainbow spelled WELCOME TO UNICORN UNIVERSITY! in big cursive letters over the party. There was a garden-gnome band playing joyful tunes on the stage, their large red pointed hats bouncing in time. Some of the unicorns were dancing to the music, while others were showing off their magical abilities—Twilight even saw one unicorn change her mane from purple to pink to teal. Clearly the other students had no trouble controlling their abilities!

Twilight did not feel as happy as the other unicorns looked. She wasn't sure where to stand or what to do. She shifted from one hoof to the other, wondering how all the other fillies and colts seemed to fit right in.

Maybe the university had made a mistake in accepting her, Twilight worried. There were schools all over Sunshine Springs, but her family always said that Unicorn University was the very best, and it was where everyone in her family had gone. But what if Twilight wasn't the best? What if she didn't belong here? She didn't have any control over her

Welcome

ability, not like the filly who could easily change the color of her mane. Twilight didn't know the moves to the dances the students were doing, and she had no idea how they could get a rainbow to spell out words. But the very worst part was that everyone was already talking and playing. It seemed like they already knew what to do.

Twilight felt a tingle begin to creep up from her hooves, as if she had stepped into a cool stream on a warm summer's day. She looked down and saw that there was only grass where her hooves should have been. It looked as if she were floating in midair.

Twilight hoped that no one noticed. She didn't want the other unicorns to think she was trying to show off her ability too! She didn't want them to think she was trying to brag, especially when she had no idea how to control her invisibility.

Twilight searched for her parents, but they were across the field, by the baskets of sugarplums, where her dad was in the middle of telling a story and making a group of unicorns laugh. Twilight wanted to run over to them to get their attention or, better yet, run home to the family farm, but her legs were frozen in place. Hot tears of frustration welled up as she felt herself plunge into full invisibility.

Twilight had just started worrying about how long she would have to be an invisible filly-shaped rock when—oof!—an adult unicorn with a multicolored mane ran right into her.

The unicorn chuckled. "Now, I know I bumped into something! But what could it be?" she asked.

Not wanting to be impolite, Twilight squeaked an embarrassed "Hello." She wished and wished she could run all the way home.

The unicorn just smiled and said, "Hello to you too!" She wore a large garland of yellow buttercups and orange poppies around her neck. Her voice was kind and her eyes were warm, and Twilight instantly felt herself relax.

Twilight could feel the tingly invisibility start to fade, replaced by the warm, welcome sunshine feeling of turning visible again. She looked down with cheer to see her purple-painted hooves appear. But she froze again when she saw that the other unicorn was looking at her quizzically.

"Welcome back!" the unicorn said. "What happened just now?" She seemed positive and kind, and it wasn't too long before Twilight found her voice again.

"I've only just discovered my magical ability," Twilight whispered. "I turn invisible when I get nervous."

The unicorn nodded. "It's hard getting used to your new power. I remember those days well. But that's part of the reason why you're here! To learn more about it and to learn to control it."

Twilight was smiling when she looked up to see her mother and father galloping over to them. She could see the concern on their faces as they got closer.

"It's not easy to find your invisible daughter," Twilight's father said, slightly out of breath.

“Professor Sherbet!” Twilight’s mother said. “Thank goodness you found Twilight. How wonderful to see you again.”

Twilight’s large gray eyes went wide in surprise. “Professor Sherbet?” she asked softly. “You wrote my letter of acceptance. You’re supposed to be my teacher!” This was not at all the stuffy, scary professor she had imagined.

Professor Sherbet nodded, her wreath of flowers shaking gently. “That’s right, Twilight! I’m excited to finally meet you. Welcome to Unicorn University.”

“Thank you, Professor,” Twilight said quietly.

“I’m very excited to learn about your new ability,” Ms. Sherbet said. “What a wonderful thing you can do!”

Twilight felt herself blush. She didn’t know what to say.

“I always find the first day and last day to be the hardest,” Professor Sherbet told her. “The first because everyone is nervous about making a good impression. And the last because no one wants to say good-bye.”

Twilight looked up at the smiling teacher. “You really think everyone is nervous?” she asked.

"I do. Even now, after many years of school and many years of teaching, I'm nervous about meeting a new class. It's always hard to start new things."

That made Twilight feel much more comfortable. Finally it seemed as if someone understood. "I have been pretty nervous about today," she said.

Ms. Sherbet smiled. "I'm sure most of the fillies and colts feel just like you do. Why don't you and your parents go check out the stables? It might make the university feel more like home. You can meet us in the Friendly Fields for our first class afterward. Once we're all gathered, I'll lead you on a tour of the school. Then I'll leave your class for the afternoon so you can create the class picture scene. I have a feeling this will be the best year yet!"

Professor Sherbet trotted off in the direction of the party as Twilight looked up at her parents. "Do you know what picture she was talking about?" she asked them.

Both parents stared back at her with their faces scrunched up. Twilight couldn't tell if they were feeling guilty or concerned. Which made her stomach drop all the way to her hooves. *What else haven't they told me about?*

"Remember, honey?" her mother said gently. "The picture that each of your sisters took on her first day of school?"

Twilight did remember. In their bedroom they each had a framed picture of their class in silly poses. Twilight had just assumed her class would do that later in the year, once they'd all gotten to know each other.

"You see," her father said, "every year the new class takes a group photo that they have to design and stage. It's a way to get to know each other. Everyone shares their ideas, and you all work together. The school always says that each unicorn is supposed to 'let their personality shine through.'"

"Each class approaches it differently," Twilight's mother explained. "My class staged it like a play where we were all acting in a big scene. It was really fun!"

"But on the first day?" Twilight squeaked, her voice much higher pitched than usual. She hadn't been planning on talking at all for at least the first week. She'd been hoping to observe and make a plan. Now she would have to let her personality shine, whatever that meant. A wave of nerves rolled over her. She wished her parents had prepared her for this.

"Don't worry, honey! You'll have fun, I promise," her mother told her.

Twilight looked up at her smiling parents. Once again she could see how excited they were for her to start school. They thought of it as an exciting new experience. How could she explain to them that it only felt like a nightmare?

"Come on," her father said. "Let's go check out the stables like Professor Sherbet suggested."

Twilight tried again to put on her bravest face. She noticed the lawn was sprinkled with little daisies, just like her lawn was back home. The familiar sight made her feel a bit better as they walked over. Soon Twilight and her parents arrived at the entrance of the stable with the sailboat twirling lazily on top.

Twilight entered her new stable with her mom and dad. It was large enough to hold forty stalls, but there was lots of light from the big windows, and the wooden floors were made of mismatched, crooked planks. It was perfectly cozy and inviting. Twilight relaxed when she found that no one else was inside. Looking around, she saw that some students had decorated their stalls with flowers, sparkling rocks, or colorful blankets. One filly had hung up a crystal that cast little rainbows everywhere.

In the acceptance letter, Professor Sherbet had included all the information Twilight would need for school. She would be staying in stall number twelve and would need to bring science goggles, a horn protector, a small cauldron, and a can of hoof ink, as well as a whole bunch of books, such as *The Beginner's Guide to Planting & Potions* and *The History of the Five Kingdoms*.

Now Twilight found the stall with a shiny golden number twelve nailed to the swinging red door. Inside were all the books and materials that her parents had sent ahead, and she saw that everything had already been carefully put away. Twilight wondered who had arranged everything so nicely. It made the stall feel a little more like her own.

Twilight's mother joined her in the stall and bobbed her head to hang her satchel on one of the stall's hooks. Using her glittering horn, she pulled a book out by its shiny brass book ring. Twilight read the title, *Little Unicorns*.

"This was my favorite book when I was your age," Twilight's mother told her, slipping the book onto the stall's book hook. "It's about three sisters, in case you ever get homesick."

Twilight felt a tear fall down her cheek. She was going to miss her parents so much.

Twilight nuzzled her mother's cheek. "Thank you," she said.

"We are very excited for you," her father said.

"And very proud," her mother added.

Twilight felt a familiar pang of worry. She didn't want to disappoint her parents. She wanted to keep making them proud.

The three unicorns huddled together in a Twilight sandwich. No one was ready, but it was time to say good-bye.

3

The Friendly Fields

Twilight left the stables before her parents. She was sure she would start to cry if she watched them walk away, and thought it was best to head straight for class after they said their good-byes.

She turned once more to wave to her parents on the way out. Their smiles and waving golden horns gave her a little confidence as she headed over to class. She tried to ignore the dancing pixies in her stomach as she walked back across the daisy-dotted knolls toward the sign for the Friendly Fields.

"Hey! Wait up!" a voice called from behind her. Twilight stopped and turned to see a mint-green colt trotting up to her. Large glasses were balanced on his nose, and his silver mane flew wildly behind him.

Twilight's chest started pounding. Had she done something wrong already?

"Hi! Are you a first year too? Are you in Ms. Sherbet's class? What's your name? My name is Shamrock!" All the words came tumbling out of his mouth as he bounced up next to her. In his excitement his glasses had gone askew, and his mane lay wildly around his shoulders.

Twilight smiled. There was something about his goofiness and excitement that reminded her of her parents' enthusiasm.

"I'm Twilight," she said. "I'm in Ms. Sherbet's class, and I'm on my way there now." The words rushed out of her so quickly that she surprised herself a little.

"Great! I can't wait for classes to start," he said. "I've been studying all summer!" He started bouncing again. "All the usual subjects of course: math, science, the history of the five kingdoms. I've been trying to learn Gnomish, but I'm afraid I said the wrong thing to the guitar player at the party. I thought I was just saying 'good job,' but I don't think I did it right. . . ."

Twilight didn't know what to say. She hadn't studied at all!

"Glimmer-foot!" Shamrock grumbled, and shook his head. "I've done it again. My dads are always telling me I have to take a breath and remember to ask other unicorns questions, not just blurt out everything I'm thinking. I'm sorry." He paused and did indeed take one deep breath, and let it out slowly. "What did you do this summer?" he asked a little more calmly.

Twilight was at a loss for words. How could she tell him that her stack of schoolbooks would make her nervous every time she looked at them, and she'd ended up covering them with a blanket? All she managed was a shrug and a frown in response.

"You know, most unicorns don't study over the summer," Shamrock went on. "They actually say in the handbook that the summer is a time for regrouping and doing what you love. I just love studying! Did you do what you love?"

Twilight smiled. She had definitely done what she loved over the summer. "I like to read and paint. And I did lots of that."

"You know how to paint?!" Shamrock exclaimed. "Could you teach me?"

Twilight thought about it. "I've never taught anyone before. But I could try."

Shamrock and Twilight followed a winding dirt path through the Wondering Woods. They could see small animals darting through the brush, and could see the bright blue sky through the trees. When they looked back, they spotted the cluster of weather vanes and the top of the Crystal Library peeking over the forest. Shamrock kept the conversation going the whole way, commenting on the school grounds and all that he'd learned about it over the summer. He didn't ask many questions, which was fine by Twilight. She was still so nervous that it felt like her tongue was a Popsicle—completely frozen.

It wasn't long before they were passing through the large wooden gates of the Friendly Fields. And it was easy to find Professor Sherbet and her flower wreath.

Twilight's stomach dropped when she noticed all the students gathered around the professor. They were too many of them!

It seemed like Shamrock was nervous too. He stopped short and looked as if he'd been scared by a ghost.

"Oh *no*! We're late!" he squeaked. "The professor is already speaking! Rule number five in the Unicorn University Handbook clearly says that students must always be on time for class. You have until the third bell rings. But I didn't hear any bell. Did you? Oh no! Do you think we're going to get expelled?"

Twilight's eyes widened, and she gulped. Expelled?

4

The Name Game

"Come! Come! You're just in time!" Professor Sherbet called from the group of unicorns.

Twilight breathed a sigh of relief and looked over to Shamrock. "Guess we're not going to be expelled just yet," she said as they walked over.

Shamrock nodded seriously. "I'm excited to be here, but I'm afraid that I'm going to do something wrong. It's all I've ever wanted, to come here and learn."

Twilight didn't know what to say. She would have liked to stay home forever.

"Welcome, Shamrock and Twilight!" Ms. Sherbet cheered as they reached the group, and everyone turned to look at them. Twilight felt her stomach pixies start dancing again. She *did not* like having all those eyes on her. “Okay. Everyone gather together,” Ms. Sherbet continued. “We’re going to play a little game to get to know each other.”

The class backed up to form a large circle, everyone’s horns pointing in. Twilight found a place between Shamrock and a sky-blue unicorn, who was talking with a rose-colored student next to her. Everyone was chatting excitedly with their neighbors.

But Twilight was not excited. She didn’t mind playing games at home. In fact, she was the undefeated champion of Pictionary in her house. But today she would have much preferred to stay quiet and listen to everyone else talk.

“This is the way it works,” Professor Sherbet went on. “Everyone introduce yourself and tell us something you love that starts with the first letter of your name. For example, my name is Professor *Sherbet*, and I love the *seashells* I find down on the *shore*.”

The rose-colored filly raised her sparkling horn and jumped a little. “Oh, Professor! How are we supposed

to choose just one? Do you think I could choose maybe three . . . or four?"

Professor Sherbet neighed merrily. "The point of the game is to help you learn each other's names. I think adding too many facts would confuse things. But I like your enthusiasm, Comet!"

Twilight was impressed. *Comet must have an amazing imagination!* Twilight wondered if Comet was an artist.

But Twilight was happy that the professor had stuck to the original plan. She was having enough trouble deciding on one thing she wanted to share, not to mention three or four! Twilight liked a lot of stuff that began with *T*, but what did she truly *love*? What thing would best describe her to her classmates?

Twilight liked the way *trees* swayed together on a windy day.

She liked when her mom would bring her a bowl of rose *tea* before bed.

She liked the *taste* of rain on hot summer days.

But which of these was the right thing to say?

Twilight was so lost in thought that she didn't realize it was her turn to speak. Shamrock gave her a little nudge.

"Oh, um—hi!" she squeaked. "My name is Twilight, and I love how ocean waves turn a special shade of *teal* when they hit the sand. The color looks just like the glass bottles that line the big window in my kitchen. I like the way colors can do that. Even when you're far away, you can still find the colors of home."

Professor Sherbet smiled at her.

The filly with a sky-blue coat and a braided royal-blue mane spoke up next. "My name is Sapphire, and I love salty seaweed!" she called out.

"My name is Comet, and I love candy!" the rose-colored unicorn said next.

As they went around the circle, Twilight felt herself shrink back. *Everyone else is choosing something simple, and I went on about teal waves,* she worried. She imagined a giant sign that said ODDBALL hanging over her head.

"Wonderful job, everyone!" Professor Sherbet told them after the last student had gone.

"It was lovely getting to know you all a little better. Perhaps it can serve as some inspiration for your class photo!"

The class started talking loudly about the class picture. It seemed like everyone but Twilight was looking forward to it.

Twilight felt as if a cloud were passing over, blocking out the sunshine. Her hooves shimmered out of sight. *Oh no! No, not now*, she thought. She squinted and tried to will the invisibility away.

"Okay. Time for the campus tour. Everyone, follow me!" The professor started galloping away, and the class quickly followed.

Twilight felt the chilly invisibility washing over her. She had totally disappeared!

"But wait!" Shamrock stopped and stretched his neck this way and that. "Where has Twilight gone?" He walked away a little to look into the woods behind him. "Twilight!" he called.

"Shamrock, shhh," Twilight whispered, trying to get him to quiet down. She did not want the rest of the group to come back and not see her like this.

Luckily, it wasn't long at all before the sunshine feeling rushed over her and she fully appeared again.

Twilight blushed. "I'm, um, right here," she told Shamrock.

He quickly turned to see her, tilting his head in surprise. "What happened?"

Twilight's shoulders slumped. "I fade out sometimes. I'm trying to get it under control."

"I don't have a magical ability yet. I wish I had one," Shamrock admitted, scuffing his front hoof on the ground.

Twilight searched for the right words but couldn't think of what to say. Not all unicorns had special abilities. Her mom didn't have one, but her dad had a special way with plants. He just knew what they needed. He always said that he could speak their language. But her mom was amazing with plants too, just in a different way. Usually unicorn abilities appeared before your first year of school, but sometimes they developed later. Twilight could see that Shamrock felt left out, but her ability caused her nothing but trouble. She would rather not have one at all.

After an awkward moment Shamrock tossed his head toward the rest of their class. "Hey, we'd better catch up with the group or we really will get expelled!"

Twilight looked after him as he trotted away. It was the first time another student had seen her ability, and she wished it had gone better. She wished she knew what she was supposed to say and do. Staying quiet was definitely not working here.

Twilight wanted to turn in the other direction and head back home, but then she thought about her parents and how excited they were for her to start school. She took a deep breath and stood a little taller, before galloping after Shamrock to join the rest of the group.

5

The Crystal Library

Twilight and Shamrock caught up with the group at the Science Stables.

"This is where we'll use our bubbling cauldrons to make healing tonics and potions," Ms. Sherbet was saying. "And in the garden behind this stable, we'll learn all about the plants of Sunshine Springs. But we have much to do today, so we'd better get going!"

Professor Sherbet dashed off again, her class trotting behind her. Twilight thought they looked like a rainbow, the herd of different-colored coats moving together.

They passed by the Gemstone Caves and the Sparkling Quarry, where the older students would have classes.

Twilight's eyes went wide when they made it to the Avocado Arena, a large flat field filled with unicorn students tossing balls and disks of different shapes and sizes between them. To her left was a big sparkling pond where unicorns splashed around. Shouts and laughter carried across the field. Twilight was amazed as she looked around. She had never been much of an athlete and knew only one or two of the games. *Does the rest of the class know how to play all these sports?* she worried.

"We call it the Avocado Arena because of the color of the grass," Professor Sherbet explained. "As you can see, it's the color of an avocado! The grass that our groundskeeper, Mr. Sorrel, uses is extra bouncy, for all the activities we'll do here. You'll all play hoofball, of course, but there are a ton of other games we'll play here as well."

Some of the class whooped in response. Twilight did not feel excited about the idea of hoofball, but she decided to worry about that another day.

"And now for our last stop on the tour. The library!" Ms. Sherbet announced. The class followed her back through the Friendly Fields, through the Wondering Woods, and across the Looping Lawn. They were out of breath when they finally arrived in front of the glimmering rainbow staircase of the Crystal Library.

It was wonderful to see the library up close. Twilight had never seen anything so large and magical. The class came to a stop before a giant, winding staircase that led up to the castle-like building. When she looked up, Twilight could spot four glittering towers on each corner. Windows of every shape were cut into the sides, and a large garden grew all around the walls. Unlike the other buildings on campus, the library wasn't made of wood. Instead it was made up of what looked like large rainbow blocks.

"I heard that this is the biggest library in the whole world!" one filly said.

"Well, that's not true. Everyone knows that the biggest library is in Soaring Spires," Sapphire told them. "This might be the biggest library in Sunshine Springs, though."

The other filly just shrugged.

Twilight was extra timid around Sapphire. Like

Shamrock, Sapphire seemed to know a ton about the school already. Way more than the rest of the class. On top of that, Sapphire didn't seem like she was afraid of anything. Twilight felt like her total opposite.

A hush came over the class as they walked up to the library. Even though they stepped carefully, you could still hear their steps clatter on the rainbow-colored stairs.

"I read in the handbook that artisans from all over the world chiseled thousands of crystals into stackable bricks to create the whole building. It's the hardest substance known to any creature, and it should stand for hundreds of thousands of years," Shamrock whispered to the group.

Twilight gasped at the spectacular doors. Each crystal reflected the light into tiny rainbows. Despite the students' muddy hooves, the stairs remained perfectly clean as the class made their way up to the intricately carved doors.

"The bricks have been enchanted to repel dirt," Shamrock said quietly. "It's another way to ensure that the building—and the books inside it—stays safe."

The sight when they walked through the large, dazzling

doors took Twilight's breath away. She could hear the other students gasp around her. Rows and rows of books circled around the building, all of them hanging by gleaming brass, golden, and silver circles. Balconies full of even more books lined the walls above their heads. Twilight could see that some unicorns were peering down from above to the floors below. The middle of the large first-floor room was filled with long rows of tables. Each table was made of shining brass and dark-colored wood. Already there were large stacks of books laid out in front of students.

For the first time that day, Twilight could picture what her life would be like here at school. She imagined coming here on a quiet afternoon and browsing through all these books. Maybe she could find a cozy corner by a window. She felt light, like she was finally at home.

The class gathered around Professor Sherbet. She had led them to the very middle of the room, where they could see everything. They all stayed perfectly quiet, even though no one had asked them to.

But the silence was soon disrupted by the clatter of

hooves on crystal. Twilight looked up to see a huge, shaggy teal unicorn with a thick raincloud-gray mane trotting toward them.

"Welcome to the library, new students!" the unicorn boomed. He grinned widely as his greeting echoed across the room. It made the whole class smile. Twilight was instantly comfortable around him, somehow. He made the place feel even more welcoming.

"Hello, Professor Jazz!" Professor Sherbet said. "Meet our newest class. Class, this is the librarian, Professor Jazz!"

"Hello, Professor Jazz!" the class said in unison.

"Hello! Hello! And welcome to my library," he boomed again.

Twilight could tell how excited he was to meet them. He bounced a little on his hooves and beamed at each student. His enthusiasm was contagious. Soon everyone was giggling and wiggling as they looked around the room.

"We have every book you could want, and if we don't, just tell me and I'll get it for you. It's my goal to be the largest library in the world!" he said.

"*Told ya,*" Sapphire whispered.

"But first let's do a little introduction." Professor Jazz swung his humongous head and gestured with his horn around the room. "All our books are arranged alphabetically by author and separated by subject. When you take out a book, be sure to tell me, and I can write it down. We like to keep track of our books here at Unicorn U."

Twilight nodded seriously. She felt so very lucky to be in this space, among all these stories. She would always treat the library with respect.

"Now, who has a book they would like to read?" Professor Jazz asked.

Sapphire's horn went right into the air. "I would like to learn how to weave the strongest nets," she said when he called on her. "My family lives by the ocean, and we like to harvest seaweed, of course. I love seaweed, but I hate fixing the ropes. Is there a book about unbreakable nets?"

"Wonderful! Wonderful!" Professor Jazz neighed happily. "This is just what the library is for. Well done, Sapphire!"

Professor Jazz's reaction made everyone start wiggling

again. Horns shot up into the air. All the students were eager to offer their questions too. Twilight even found herself wanting to ask him something. *Maybe there's a book about escaping the class picture*, she thought.

Professor Sherbet neighed in her merry way. "Let's start with this question. You'll have plenty of time to come back," she told them.

"Now, let me think." Professor Jazz tapped his left hoof a few times on the sparkling floor. "First we'll have to find you the strongest rope, which I believe is the Spider Fairy's thread. Though, we will have to confirm. . . . Hmm. Let's get the complete guide to fairy thread to be sure. Then we'll need a weaving book as well. Follow me! Follow me!"

The class followed behind Professor Jazz as he led them to a corner of the library. Twilight hung toward the back of the group, wanting to linger and look closely at everything. She peered down the aisles of books and listened to the muffled chatter of students all around her. *How magical*, she thought.

She caught up with the class in time to see Professor Jazz

using his horn to get a large purple book with painted fairy wings on the spine. Then he led the group down another aisle to get a faded blue book with the word "weaving" printed in big block letters on the cover.

Both books hung from gleaming silver rings that now circled his horn.

"I think this will be a good place to start!" He trotted toward the large desk at the back of the library, with the class following quickly behind.

Professor Jazz went behind the desk to a shining silver hook. A little plaque above it said SAPPHIRE. He dipped his horn to slide the books onto the hook. Then he turned back toward the group.

"You all have a hook back here, and if you ever need to put a book on hold, just ask me and it will be waiting for you. After the tour, Sapphire, you can come back and check these out for your project. I'll search for other books in the meantime."

Twilight looked at the wall and spotted her own name above a silver hook. It was like all the other plaques, just a simple silver rectangle. But it gave her a thrill to see her name up there. It made her feel like she might belong here after all.

"Thank you, Mr. Jazz!" Professor Sherbet said. "Now, class, follow me outside—it's time for lunch!"

6

Class Picnic

The Peony Pasture was a large orchard covered with apple trees and, of course, peonies. The older unicorns were gathered in groups around the field, grazing on grass and munching apples. The whole pasture was abuzz with the sounds of neighing, laughter, and excited chatter. Shamrock was talking with Comet and Sapphire as they followed Ms. Sherbet through the trees, and all their other classmates were giggling and discussing the day with each other.

Twilight suddenly felt very small. She was the only one not excited and chatting away. Twilight just felt panicked and sweaty.

Professor Sherbet ushered them over to an open spot under

an old apple tree. She reached up and used her horn to shake a bunch of apples loose. "Eat up, fillies and colts! We have a big afternoon ahead of us, and I want you all to have a good lunch."

"Because of the school pictures?" Shamrock asked. He already had a big bite of grass, and some of the strands were hanging out of his mouth as he talked. "I know all about them from the handbook," he added.

"That's right, Shamrock!" Professor Sherbet told him. "It's a tradition here at Unicorn U to create a unique and memorable picture. You should all get to know each other and work together to create something really special. Every year we give our students one direction: let each student's personality shine through. This exercise is a great way to get to know one another."

Twilight felt the stomach pixies, and they were tap-dancing this time. She had hoped Ms. Sherbet would forget about the class picture. Or say that some unicorns could just stand awkwardly in the background, maybe with their faces hidden behind a tree.

"What have your other classes done?" Sapphire asked. "That would help us think of some ideas."

Once again Twilight was impressed by how comfortable Sapphire was about taking charge. Twilight doubted that Sapphire would have any trouble letting her personality shine. It sparkled naturally.

"I'm not going to tell you!" Professor Sherbet told them. She laughed when the class started grumbling. "I want you all to approach this with fresh eyes. It's the first thing you're going to do together as a class. Have fun with it! Be silly and take chances! I want you all to try your best and get involved. After lunch, brainstorm ideas for the picture, and meet me back in front of the library after the end-of-day bell."

Twilight's heart was pounding so hard, she could feel it in her ears. What was she going to do?

★

The class started talking as soon as Ms. Sherbet trotted away. Everyone seemed to have an idea for the picture and was trying to make their voice heard. Twilight inched back toward the edge of the group, desperate to run away.

"Let's make a unicorn pyramid," Comet called out. "I saw it once at the circus! It was amazing! Okay, someone try to get onto my back!"

But instead of kneeling down, her rose-colored hooves started floating off the ground. Comet had the gift of flight!

"Oh no, not now." Comet groaned. "Could someone pull me down? Just grab my tail."

But the class wasn't listening. Everyone was still trying to get their class picture ideas heard. Twilight might have wanted to hide in the stables, but she could understand what Comet was going through and quickly went over and pulled Comet down by her tail, just as Comet had asked.

"Oof, thank you!" Comet said when she landed firmly on the ground. "That would have been really embarrassing if everyone had been paying attention." She laughed and

stomped her hooves, as if to make sure she was really standing again.

Twilight nodded. She totally got that.

Comet laughed nervously. "I mean, um, I totally have control over it. It's only sometimes that, well . . . I don't."

Twilight searched for the right words to make Comet feel better. This was something her sister Sunset was always good at, joking and making unicorns feel good. Twilight didn't want to make the same mistake that she had with Shamrock and not say anything at all.

Comet just giggled at the silence. "You're Twilight, right?" she asked. "I'm Comet."

Twilight nodded and squeaked, "I remember."

"Did you like my idea about the unicorn pyramid?" Comet asked.

Twilight thought it would be cool and also very scary. But she worried that saying this would make Comet feel bad. So she just went with a shrug.

"I think it takes a lot of practice and coordination . . . ," Comet said. "And maybe we're not there yet."

Twilight looked over at the squabbling class.

"Did you have any ideas?" Comet asked.

Twilight didn't know how to explain to Comet that she was too scared of this project—and, well, everyone—to even try to think of any ideas.

Comet raised her eyebrows as the silence stretched on. Twilight knew she needed to say *something*, but the more she tried to think of the right thing, the more frozen she felt.

"Okay, well, guess I'd better get back to everyone else," Comet said finally. "Thank you for helping me down. Sorry to ask so many questions. I didn't mean to bother you." Comet quickly trotted over to the group.

Twilight felt her heart sink all the way to her hooves. She'd done it again! Why couldn't she ever think of the right thing to say? Or think of anything to say at all?

Now Twilight didn't feel nervous. She just felt sad.

It felt like all the things she'd worried about were actually happening. She hadn't known the right thing to say all day and had offended the only two classmates she'd talked to! Twilight desperately wanted to go back home. She decided she'd rather disappoint her parents than keep hurting unicorns' feelings.

7

Surprise!

Twilight's heart was heavy when she arrived at the stables, but she was relieved to find the stables empty. Her class was still brainstorming, and everyone else was still out at lunch or exploring the grounds. She thought of all she had seen that day and was sad that she wouldn't get to know the library as she had hoped. But she didn't want to do one more wrong thing. A few hot tears fell down her cheeks as she imagined her parents' disappointed faces.

Twilight quickly spotted stall number twelve. She walked over to her little shelf to start packing her belongings, and found her paint satchel first. The satchel was made of old tan leather and could fold out into an easel. It could

hang comfortably from her neck, and she could take it anywhere she went.

The satchel had belonged to Grandmother Stardust. When Twilight had been young, her grandmother had traveled the five kingdoms to paint. Grandmother Stardust had given Twilight the satchel full of paints before Twilight started school, saying that her granddaughter was destined to have many great adventures and would need the right tools.

More tears fell down Twilight's face. She would write her grandmother a note and return the paints as soon as she was home.

But before she had a chance to slip the satchel onto her neck, Twilight heard a noise from outside the stall. First it was just hums and gurgles, but then she heard beautiful singing. It was "Somewhere over the Stars," a song she used to sing with her sisters all the time! It felt like a little bit of home had landed in the stables, making her feel suddenly safe. Carefully Twilight snuck out of the stall to investigate. She crept toward the front of the barn, peering into each stall, until she caught a flash of blue.

It was Sapphire! She was swaying inside one of the stalls, her long, braided blue mane swishing in time.

Suddenly Twilight felt like she knew the perfect thing to say. *I'm heading home anyway*, she thought.

Might as well say something before I leave.

"You have the most beautiful voice. It reminds me of stepping into the sunshine," Twilight said almost confidently.

Sapphire stopped singing and sharply spun around to face Twilight. "I thought I was alone!" she screeched.

Twilight felt her stomach drop, as if it were suddenly full of a thousand crystal bricks. She backed away full of regret.

For the first time since her power had appeared, Twilight was happy to feel the familiar tingle of invisibility. She could not disappear fast enough.

"Twilight?" Sapphire asked, her voice squeaking with concern. "Twilight? Where'd you go? I'm sorry I was rude. I just don't usually sing in front of others. And, well, I don't think I'm very good at it. I just like to do it." She dug at the floor with one of her hooves. "But that is the nicest thing anyone has ever said to me. I was just surprised!"

Now *Twilight* was surprised. Sapphire had seemed so very confident.

"Today has been kind of a hard day," Sapphire continued.

Invisible Twilight let out a long breath. *The day has been hard for other unicorns?* she wondered. *I thought it was just me.* "For me too," she admitted quietly, surprising herself.

"Yeah? I have four younger sisters, and I'm used to taking charge . . . ," Sapphire said. "It felt like everyone thought I was really bossy, though."

Twilight was impressed. It made her feel good that Sapphire could tell Twilight something so personal. She wanted to say the right thing to make Sapphire feel better but felt at a loss once more. She let the pause stretch out.

"Oh, okay. I get it." Sapphire sighed. "I'll go now."

Twilight saw that Sapphire's eyes were brimming with tears as she brushed by her.

Twilight did not want to offend another unicorn today. She desperately wanted to help.

"Wait!" Twilight croaked. "I didn't think you were bossy! I've been nervous all day, and you seemed so *confident*. I have two older sisters, and actually, you kind of remind me of them."

Sapphire stopped short. Then her face broke out in a big smile. "Thanks, Twilight."

Twilight remembered that earlier in the day she had thought she and Sapphire were opposites. Now she felt like she understood Sapphire a little more. Well, until she saw Sapphire turning circles in the barn, looking up and down the rows of stalls. Twilight was about to laugh when she realized what Sapphire was looking for.

"Oh, I'm right over here," Twilight called from the hallway outside Sapphire's stall.

Sapphire laughed. "Huh? Where?" she asked. "Are you hiding?"

"I've gone invisible," Twilight said, only a little flustered. Sapphire had been so honest with her that it felt a little easier to be honest back. "Sometimes it happens when I get embarrassed or nervous. I should be reappearing again soon, now that you've noticed. I try to turn visible again myself, but it usually takes someone else realizing that I've disappeared."

Sapphire just nodded. "I guess we were both embarrassed."

Twilight nodded too, before she remembered again that

Sapphire couldn't see that. "Totally," she said. She looked down at her hooves, expecting to see her hooficure appear once more.

But . . . nothing was happening.

Twilight closed her eyes and tried to focus on the sunshine feeling that came with turning visible again. But all she could feel were the cool waves of invisibility.

"Oh no," Twilight whinnied, suddenly very nervous.

"Twilight? What's wrong?" Sapphire asked.

"Um, well . . . I have no idea," Twilight admitted, her voice quivering. "I usually start reappearing again by now."

Sapphire nodded again in understanding. "Don't worry. You'll appear again! You're not the first unicorn at school with this gift. I'm sure there's an explanation!"

Sapphire sounded so sure that it made Twilight's spirits lift a little. But despite all of Sapphire's confidence, Twilight was still invisible, and neither of them had a clue why. She looked over to her stall and saw her half-packed bag. Her stomach sank further.

"That's the thing. I don't think I belong at school,"

Twilight admitted sadly. "Clearly I can't control my power. I always say the wrong thing." Twilight felt lower than she had all day, and tears flooded down her cheeks. She took a deep breath. "I just need to go home."

Sapphire's eyes went wide, and her jaw dropped open in surprise. Then she cocked her head with a big smile. Twilight wiggled, worrying about what Sapphire was going to say.

"But I came in here thinking the same thing!" Sapphire said. "I felt like running home too. I was singing and thinking about packing up my stuff."

Now it was Twilight's eyes that went wide. "But you belong here more than anyone else!" Twilight finally managed.

Sapphire just shook her head, still smiling. "Actually, I think we all belong here. It's only, well, first days are hard. You should totally stay, Twilight."

Twilight blushed happily. Even though her mind had been made up, she felt better hearing Sapphire's words. "You can't even see me, Sapphire," Twilight reminded her. "I mean, think about the class picture. How is my personality supposed to show when you can't even see me?"

Sapphire bit her bottom lip and squinted her eyes a little. "You can't go home when you're invisible, right? That would be super dangerous. I mean, what if you got lost? How would we find you?"

Twilight hadn't even thought about that. "That's true," she said.

"Okay, then," Sapphire went on. "Wait until after the class picture. If you decide you still want to go home, you can tell Ms. Sherbet. But until then, you have to stay here and let me help you become visible."

Twilight thought it over. The plan did make her feel a little better. It would be a lot less embarrassing to figure out the invisibility thing before going to Professor Sherbet.

"Okay, deal," Twilight told her.

"Deal." Sapphire nodded in determination. "We may need some help, though. Let me go get Comet—"

"Did someone say 'COMET'?!"

Sapphire and Twilight looked up to see Comet striking a dramatic pose in the doorway. She flung her mane out and pointed her horn, as if she were posing at a fashion show.

Twilight started to panic. Their last conversation had been such a disaster. What would Comet do when she discovered that Twilight was there too?

"Comet! Great timing," Sapphire told her. "Come over here."

Comet half floated, half trotted over to them. She skidded to a stop in front of Sapphire and almost ran right into invisible Twilight.

"Hi, Comet," Twilight said softly.

"Twilight! Is that you?" Comet exclaimed. "Are you invisible or something?"

"Yeah." Twilight hung her invisible horn. "It's my ability. But I have absolutely no control over it. And, well, now I can't turn back."

"Oh no!" Comet exclaimed. "Ugh. I know that feeling. I was totally lying before—I always need someone to help me down once I start floating. One time I flew all the way to the top of a super-tall tree and couldn't get down. Luckily, my uncle can fly too and got me down."

Twilight's heart swelled. "Actually," she said, "I wanted to tell you about my invisibility problems before, but I just got all tongue-tied. I'm sorry if I made you feel bad."

"Oh, glitterplat!" Comet said, waving her horn. "I was worried that I was bothering you. I feel like I've been bugging everyone all day. I always talk a lot when I get nervous. Or, actually, I talk a lot all the time." Comet paused and laughed.

Twilight was stunned. Both Comet and Sapphire had been nervous too?

"Anyway, I'm super grateful that you helped me down," Comet said. "So, how can *I* help *you*?"

Twilight smiled, despite the fact that she was totally panicked and astonished. It was a weird feeling.

"Glad you asked," Sapphire said. She shook her braided mane and stomped twice. "I think we should go to the library!"

Hope swept through Twilight like a gust of summer wind. Sapphire was right. Surely one of the books in such a calm, sparkling place would have the answer.

"That is the perfect plan!" Comet said.

"I know it is," Sapphire said with a grin.

But Twilight was nervous. She didn't want the whole school to find out she was stuck as an invisible unicorn! "Do you think we could keep this whole invisibility problem a secret?" she asked.

"I love secret missions!" Comet cheered. "But, uh, why does it have to be secret?"

Twilight dug at the wood floors, creating tiny puffs of dust that seemed to appear out of nowhere. "I'm just embarrassed. I don't want everyone to know I'm stuck this way. They'll think I'm some sort of scary ghost."

"I don't think they will, Twilight," Sapphire said. "But we can still keep it a secret. *And* we're going to get you into the class picture, *and* convince you to stay!"

Comet pranced around with excitement. "Brava! Sapphire, you are totally and completely right. Twilight must stay! We all have to! And I will totally help you convince her. And keep it a secret if that's what you want."

Twilight was stunned. For what felt like the billionth time that day, Twilight felt tears well up in her eyes. But this time they were the happy kind. She didn't know if she could really stay at the school forever, but she could at least stay until the end of the day. "Thanks, you guys," she finally said.

"Woo-hoo! Library Secret Mission: Operation Visible," Comet cheered.

8

The Light Idea

The library was filled with students looking at books in the aisles and reading at the large tables in the front. Sapphire, ignoring all the hustle and bustle, marched straight up to Mr. Jazz.

Twilight followed behind. It was difficult to weave her way through all the students when she was invisible. Every time she said "Excuse me," a filly or colt would just look around and then shrug when they didn't see anyone there.

"Mr. Jazz!" Sapphire yelled over the chattering students, waving her horn so he would notice them.

"Hello there!" Mr. Jazz yelled back when he spotted them. Well, when he spotted Comet and Sapphire. "Have you come to pick up your books for the fishing nets? I've added a few more to the pile." Mr. Jazz gestured over to her hook, where about a dozen books now hung.

"No, no. This is much more important," Sapphire said impatiently. "We need some books on unicorn invisibility, please."

"Now, why would you need that?" Mr. Jazz asked.

Twilight froze, and her heart started racing at lightning-bird speed. *Will he figure it out?*

Luckily, Comet was a quick thinker. "Because I've just discovered my magical ability. And I want to learn about other unicorn abilities too," she told him.

Mr. Jazz looked puzzled. Then he shrugged and said, "Well, you're in luck! One of your classmates is already over there with lots of different books about magical abilities. And he has some books on invisibility too."

Comet, Sapphire, and Twilight looked over and saw Shamrock in the corner standing by a table, with books piled all around him. He was peering over his large, black-rimmed glasses, lost in the pages in front of him.

The three fillies thanked Mr. Jazz and walked over to Shamrock. "It's okay," Twilight whispered. "We can tell Shamrock." She had been able to get over her awkwardness with Sapphire and Comet, so maybe she could try again with Shamrock, too.

"Shamrock!" Comet exclaimed loudly. "We super need your help!"

"Uh, Comet, maybe don't say that quite so loudly," Twilight whispered, worried others would hear.

Shamrock whipped his head around so fast that his glasses went askew. "Twilight? Where are you?"

Sapphire rolled her eyes. "She's invisible, as you can't see. That's why we need your help." She used her horn to straighten his glasses for him.

"Oh, okay," Shamrock said.

"She can't turn back," Comet explained further. "And we were hoping one of these books could help. We've got to turn her back before the class picture!"

"Of course," Shamrock agreed. "You can't miss the class picture! The school handbook says—"

"Nope!" Sapphire interrupted him. "This is not about any school rules. This is about showing Twilight she belongs here."

"She wants to go home, and we want her to stay, obviously," Comet explained.

Twilight squirmed uncomfortably. It felt odd having all this attention on her, especially since no one could see her.

Shamrock looked at Sapphire, then at Comet. After a brief pause, he nodded in his serious way.

"Of course you need to stay, Twilight! You're going to help me learn to paint! And if that requires keeping your secret from the teachers, well . . ."

Sapphire, Comet, and Twilight held their breath as they waited for his decision.

"Then we can forget about the handbook!"

Sapphire and Comet whooped and cheered, and Twilight squirmed some more. She had not expected the day to go like this.

"Woo-hoo!" Comet cheered again. "Best first day ever! And I thought the class picture would be my favorite part of the day."

"Oh yeah. What theme did the class decide on?" Sapphire asked.

"No one could agree on anything, so we all just decided to show up with props for different ideas. We can decide right before the picture," Shamrock said, filling them in. "That's why I'm here, actually. I thought we might do something that represents different unicorn magical abilities. Did you know that our powers come from the Four Magical Elements? Every ability is somehow related to water, light, air, or earth."

"I didn't know that," Twilight said. "I guess Comet's flight comes from the air? What about invisibility?"

Shamrock wiggled. He was clearly excited about this question.

"From light, of course," Sapphire told them.

Shamrock nodded enthusiastically. "Exactly!" he said. "And, actually, I think that might be the key to turning Twilight back!"

9

Under the Rainbow

"Come on!" Shamrock urged. "Follow me!"

The three fillies followed him out of the library and cantered over to the Looping Lawn. The gnome band had packed up, and the candied apples were nowhere in sight. But the welcome rainbow still hung merrily above their heads.

"Okay," Shamrock said, and they stopped. The four of them panted for a moment, trying to catch their breath. "Sapphire was right: invisibility comes from the magical element of light. And the biggest source of light is sunlight. And here we have a rainbow—"

"And rainbows are refracted light!" Sapphire shouted.

“Uh, guys, what does that mean?” Comet asked.

“It’s when a light beam bends as it moves from one thing into another. Like when sunlight goes through air and then hits water,” Shamrock explained, sounding very professor-like.

While Comet, Sapphire, and Shamrock went on discussing rainbows and light, Twilight’s mind began to wander. She wondered what life would be like if she were invisible forever. She imagined herself living like a ghost in her house, having to knock things over and howl to be noticed. Her heart began to pound, and she tried to take a deep breath to calm down. She liked being quiet, but totally forgotten? That would be the worst.

Twilight noticed Shamrock walking over to a giant water bubble that was spurting out the rainbow sign. She decided she had better pay attention. They were trying to help her, after all.

“So the light from the sun is being refracted through the big raindrop over here,” he was saying.

“I’m guessing that a unicorn with a magical water

ability and a unicorn with a magical sunlight ability worked together to create this. Or maybe one unicorn with a magical rainbow ability?" Shamrock wondered aloud.

"Right." Sapphire nodded, clearly trying to get him back on track. "So you're thinking, if Twilight runs through the rainbow here, the refracted light should make her visible again?" Sapphire asked.

"Exactly!" Shamrock yelled. He and Sapphire tapped their horns together in a high-U.

Twilight felt her spirits lift, as if her heart had Comet's gift of flight. "Thank you so much for helping me with this. I was starting to worry that I was going to be invisible forever."

"You totally won't be!" Comet cheered. "We've got this."

Twilight took a deep breath. "Okay. So I just run through the rainbow and I'll reappear, right?"

The other three fillies and colts nodded.

Twilight took another steadying breath and stood a little taller. Even though no one could see her, she wanted to run through this magical rainbow with confidence.

"Okay. Here I go!" Twilight ran back and forth through

the ribbons of colors. She ran through on one side, where the rainbow started and was close to the ground. Then she jumped up so the rainbow would touch her face. Jumping through a rainbow was unlike anything she had done before. It was incredible. She jumped higher than ever, lifted by the possibility of turning back to her old self.

Finally Twilight trotted back toward the group, excited to see the looks on their faces.

10

The Mystery

Twilight still felt the cool waves of invisibility, and looked down to find that her legs had not reappeared. The four unicorns groaned in unison. Jumping through the rainbow hadn't worked.

Twilight's poor stomach had been flipping up and down all day, and now it seemed as if it were somewhere by her invisible hooficured hooves.

If the others could have seen her, they would have seen that Twilight's head hung so low that her horn touched the grass. A few tears fell down her cheeks.

"Thank you so much for trying to help me with this," Twilight told them. "But I don't want to cause you guys any more trouble. You should be getting ready for the class picture! I know you three will think of a great idea for it. I'm just going to go tell Professor Sherbet that it's time for me to go home."

Shamrock looked down bashfully. "You know, I was worried I didn't belong here today either. That's why I kept bringing up the handbook! I thought that if I knew the school rules, then I would know how to be a student. But trying to figure this out has made me realize that Sapphire is right. We all belong here because we can help each other, you know?"

"Yes!" Comet shouted. "I still think this has been the best first day ever. We have this mystery we have to solve together!"

Soon Comet, Sapphire, and Shamrock started shouting silly ideas to solve the "mystery."

Twilight was taken aback and realized . . . they were right. It did feel like she was part of something. She started laughing along with them. "If only I had enough paint to just . . . repaint myself," she said.

Shamrock and Sapphire giggled, but Comet started floating.

"Wait! That gives me an idea." Comet had a huge smile on her face. "Sugar!"

But all she saw were two puzzled looks. Of course, Twilight looked puzzled too, but Comet couldn't see it.

"Uh, Comet, what do you mean by that?" Twilight asked kindly.

"We can cover you in powdered sugar!" she explained.

Twilight had only ever had powdered sugar on candied apples. How could it help a unicorn? But the others looked at each other and nodded seriously.

"Great idea," Shamrock said. "Powdered sugar is sticky enough to stay on."

"True," Sapphire agreed. "I wonder if being able to be seen will bring back your visibility. Like a mind trick or something."

Shamrock nodded his horn. "Brilliant. Only, how do we get all that powdered sugar?" he asked.

"From the kitchens, of course!" Comet told them. "The

campus chefs said that every Friday they make those candied apples that we had this morning at the welcome picnic. So they must have tons of sugar."

"How do you know that, Comet?" Shamrock wondered.

"Because I asked! Those candied apples were the best I've ever had, so I went looking for the recipe. Technically, you're not supposed to go into the kitchen . . . but I consider that more of a suggestion than a rule," Comet told them with an eyebrow wiggle that made them all laugh.

"But don't you think Professor Sherbet will think it's strange when Twilight shows up covered in powdered sugar?" Shamrock asked.

"Not if everyone else is covered in powdered sugar too," Sapphire suggested.

"Huh? Why would that help?" Twilight asked.

"Because it's our class picture idea, of course!" Sapphire told her.

Twilight wasn't as sure as the rest of the group was. Could covering herself in sugar really bring back her visibility? But everyone was excited and happy about the plan,

and she didn't want to spoil it for them. And maybe if they did get the powdered sugar, the class picture wouldn't be so bad. Maybe, just maybe, it might be fun to stand there with these three. She still wasn't sure about the whole school thing, but being part of a group photo of frosted unicorns didn't sound like the worst idea.

"Let's do it," Twilight said.

"Great!" Sapphire was clearly excited. "Shamrock, you go tell the class what's going on. Twilight, you okay with bringing in the other students?"

Twilight's stomach pixies did a few flips. She still didn't like the idea of being the center of attention, but she didn't want to disappoint these magical unicorns who were trying so hard to help her. And that meant they would have to tell the class the plan.

"No problem," Twilight said.

11

Stella and Celest

While Shamrock went to tell the others, Sapphire and Twilight followed Comet to the kitchens. They wove through the Peony Pasture, where some students were still grazing, but no one thought anything of the two first-year fillies walking by.

Finally they reached a large, moss-covered building next to a giant oak tree. The walls of the building were made of stitched bark, and a chimney made of smooth white pebbles twisted out of the rounded roof. Little tufts of gray smoke puffed out.

Comet walked confidently to the front door, which was low and wide and painted the same red as the school barns.

"How many times have you been here?" Sapphire asked.

"Oh, only the one time earlier today. But it was wonderful," Comet told them. She knocked three times with her horn, and the door opened to reveal a small green dragon wearing a bright blue apron.

"Comet! Back again so soon?" The dragon's voice sounded like a million flutes playing in unison. Twilight had never met a dragon before. She was surprised that its voice was so musical. She made a mental note to ask Sunset about this later.

The dragon opened the door wider and moved aside to let them in. The inside was bright, with blue-checkered curtains and cheery yellow walls. Twilight loved it immediately. It reminded her of her home on the farm.

A gray speckled unicorn was using her long horn to stir something in a giant black cauldron in the center of the room. "Don't mind me!" she called. "I have to stir this a hundred times or it will turn to mush. Just a moment!"

"Well, in the meantime, why don't you introduce your friends, Comet?" the dragon asked.

Twilight wiggled with excitement. Had she become visible again? She was so surprised and excited that she almost knocked over a shelf full of spices!

"Wait. *Friends?* How do you know that Comet has brought more than one friend?" Sapphire asked.

Twilight's shoulders sank with disappointment. *Still invisible, I guess. But how does the dragon know I'm here?*

“Ahh, dragons have some magic of their own, little one,” the dragon said with a wink.

“One hundred!” the unicorn at the cauldron shouted. “Phew, this recipe is always tricky.” She wiped her horn on the checkered cloth hanging on the wall. Her wire-rimmed glasses were still a little foggy from the cauldron’s steam. “My name is Celest. And this mysterious dragon is Stella.”

“Pleased to meet you all!” Stella said with a nod and a grin.

“Stella, Celest. These are my friends, Sapphire—”

Comet paused to motion toward Sapphire, who waved her horn and said, “Hello!”

“And this . . . ,” Comet continued, looking around the room. “Well, actually, Twilight, where are you?”

“Over here by the door,” Twilight said. “It’s nice to meet you both,” she said to Stella and Celest.

“So, we have an invisible filly in our kitchens, huh?” Celest asked.

“We were hoping for some help,” Comet told them. “You see, I remembered how you told me about the candied apples recipe, and well . . .”

Suddenly Comet seemed at a loss for words. She looked down at her hooves, as if nervous to ask for such a big favor. Twilight was shocked. She hadn't thought Comet could ever run out of words!

Sapphire started to speak. "Yes, you see, um, we would need, um . . ." Her voice trailed off, as if she couldn't ask them for all that sugar either.

The two unicorns had helped Twilight a lot that day, so she thought it was time she came to their rescue. She took a deep breath and said, "We were wondering if we could take some of your powdered sugar."

"Actually, we'll need a lot of powdered sugar," Sapphire said, finding her voice. "Enough to cover our whole class with it."

They were all silent for a moment. Then Stella and Celest burst out laughing.

"I'm guessing this has something to do with class pictures?" Celest finally said, once she had recovered.

The three fillies nodded.

Celest tapped her hoof on the ground, and Stella

scratched her scaly head with one long, purple-painted claw. Then they looked at each other for a long time, as if chatting silently. Twilight wondered if that was actually what they were doing.

"Okay, here's what we can do," Stella finally told them. "You can have one bag. We need the sugar for our recipes, and I think it would be a waste to just dump all of it out. But we can spare one bag, and it should cover one unicorn filly, which is all you really need, anyway. Right?"

"Well, actually—" Comet started to say, but Sapphire interrupted.

"Deal," she said.

"All right, but you have to make us a promise," Celest said.

Twilight bit her lip. What kind of bargain would they have to make?

"You have to send us a copy of the picture!" Stella said. She and Celest burst out laughing again.

The fillies joined in with them. It was a silly plan, after all. Twilight might have been just an invisible unicorn with an odd plan, but, she suddenly realized, she had made some wonderful friends on this strange day. And with that thought, she wondered if going home was quite the right thing to do after all.

★

The three fillies borrowed some rope from Celest and Stella before they left the kitchen. By tying the rope to the bag and then around their waists, Sapphire and Comet were able to drag the large bag of powdered sugar behind them. Twilight wanted to help, but everyone agreed that a rope hanging in midair would cause suspicion.

On the way back, Twilight smiled as she listened to her new friends laugh and chat. Unicorn U didn't feel scary anymore. It was actually really fun. And Twilight couldn't stop thinking about how she wanted to be a student here after all.

But then Twilight remembered she was still invisible. What if she was like this forever? Would the school even allow her to stay? Her heart pounded at the thought.

"We're almost there, guys," Sapphire said, interrupting

Twilight's spiral of worries. "Operation Visible is almost complete."

Twilight smiled. "Thank you for all your help, you guys. This day has been way better than I thought it would be. And I really want to stay here at Unicorn U."

Comet and Sapphire whooped and cheered. They bounced so much that some powdered sugar escaped in little sparkly puffs.

"But I don't think they'll let an invisible filly hang around . . . ," Twilight admitted when they'd calmed down. A few invisible tears fell down her invisible checks.

"It's going to be okay, Twilight," Sapphire said, still as confident as ever. "If the sugary mind trick doesn't work, then we'll just tell Professor Sherbet. She'll know what to do."

"You're not going anywhere, Twilight!" Comet said.

★

They met up with Shamrock, who was pacing back and forth under the rainbow banner.

"Shamrock!" Comet called out to him.

Twilight could see a look of relief fall over his face when he saw them. Then he saw at the bag of powdered sugar, and his face scrunched up again. "You guys! I thought you were going to get enough sugar for everyone?"

"Well, turns out that's a lot of sugar, and Stella and Celest couldn't part with all of it," Comet told him with a shrug.

The group paused. Twilight realized that the three fillies had just been happy with the experience of getting the sugar. They hadn't even thought of how this would affect the over-all plan. Twilight, of course, started to panic.

"Oh, don't worry. I have a way better plan!" Sapphire said.

12

Sugar Time

"Okay. You ready, Twilight?" Comet yelled from the top of the hill.

Twilight waited at the bottom of the hill next to the blueberry bush, just as they had planned. She breathed in and out slowly, preparing herself for the next step. "Ready!" she called back.

Comet ran down the hill, and then—suddenly—a rose-colored blur flew right over Twilight, showering her in sparkling powdered sugar. Twilight giggled as the sugary sweetness covered her completely.

"Oof!" Comet landed just beyond her with a hard thud. "Did you see that?" she bellowed. "I totally made that

landing! That was the coolest! Should we do it again?"

Twilight chuckled. "You're fearless!"

Sapphire and Shamrock came cantering down the hill, whooping and hollering with glee. Just as they reached the sugary mess at the bottom of the hill, a loud bell rang out, followed by a chorus of birds chirping, "End of class! End of class!"

Sapphire laughed. "Professor Sherbet was right. You really can't miss that bell. Hurry, guys. We still have to finish getting ready for the picture!"

★

The class assembled on the library's front steps. Shamrock had done a good job spreading the word about the change in plans.

Ms. Sherbet came galloping over to them, neighing in her joyful, merry way. "Well, everyone! I think this is the most impressive class picture I've ever seen. You guys have really done something unique."

The class giggled together and shared secretive looks.

"Can you guess the theme, Professor?" Sapphire asked.

"Well, hmm . . ." Professor Sherbet thought for a minute before shaking her head. "I have to admit, I have no idea! Will you tell me?"

"We're in disguise!" Comet yelled.

"We call this the Mystery Picture," Twilight explained, smiling wide. She was so happy, she could burst. She felt like a totally different unicorn from the one who'd played the name game earlier that day.

Professor Sherbet neighed merrily again. "Wonderful! Wonderful!"

Twilight looked around at her fellow classmates. "Mystery Picture" described the scene perfectly. Everyone had covered themselves head to toe with something different. Comet had flown up to pull down the branches of a newly blooming tree and covered herself with bright yellow pollen. She looked like a ray of sunshine. Shamrock was dressed as a gnome. He'd used a red blanket for a cape and had found a red cap that a gnome had left behind, and he'd topped it off with a fake beard. Sapphire had woven a blanket out of vines and leaves and thrown it over herself. She'd copied one of the easier designs from a library book. And all the other classmates had creatively disguised themselves as well. Despite being hidden, it still felt like everyone's personalities shone through. It was the coolest.

After the picture, Ms. Sherbet told them it was time for dinner and then it was off to bed. Comet, Sapphire, and Shamrock tossed off their disguises and trotted away in the direction of the Looping Lawn.

Twilight watched them leave. She felt frozen. She couldn't toss her disguise off so easily. If she washed off the powdered sugar, she would be invisible again.

There was nothing left to do. It was time to talk to Professor Sherbet. Twilight would tell her all about the invisibility, but after the day she'd had, Twilight knew she belonged at Unicorn U with her friends. Thinking about everything that had happened made her feel like she was drinking a cup of cocoa with extra marshmallows and whipped cream. She just had to tell Ms. Sherbet the truth. The professor would understand. Twilight wiggled and wiggled and let the powdered sugar fall off.

"Twilight! Twilight!" Sapphire called over.

Twilight looked up and saw that Sapphire, Comet, and Shamrock were looking over at her, waiting for her to join them. *But wait*, Twilight thought. *They're looking right at me. How do they know where to look?*

Twilight looked down and started jumping for joy. She could see her purple-painted hooves shining through the left-over powdered sugar! And her jet-black coat, too! Twilight couldn't stop laughing and dancing.

"Whoa! Why so excited?" asked the unicorn who'd taken the class picture.

Normally Twilight would be embarrassed and would fade out. But she was so happy that she didn't care who saw her crazy dance moves.

"I think I can finally see myself," she told him. Then she had an exciting idea. "Hey, would you mind taking another picture? One of me and my friends?"

"Sure can!" the photographer agreed.

★

A week later Twilight added one more thing to stall number twelve. It was a wooden frame that held the photo of her with Shamrock, Comet, and Sapphire. The four unicorn fil-lies and colts smiled broadly, powdered sugar smudged on all their faces.

Twilight took a step back to admire the scene. *I'm so lucky to have friends like these,* she thought. *I can't wait for all the adventures to come!*

READ ON FOR A PEEK AT

Sapphire's

SEARCH FOR HER OWN SPECIAL MAGIC!

Sapphire's Special Power

Sapphire was so excited that she couldn't stop moving. It felt like her hooves were filled with dancing beans. She dashed among her fellow first years of Unicorn University, making sure everyone was ready to go. They were all gathered together on the Looping Lawn, under the two tallest oak trees. The large knobbly branches stretched out far above them, covering the rainbow cluster of unicorn students.

Sapphire noticed that the sun was lower in the sky. She straightened her shoulders and shook her long, braided blue mane. “Okay!” she shouted to get everyone’s attention. “Let’s get into our places. Shamrock, Firefly, you guys head across the field to make sure the banner is high enough so that Fairy Green can see it when she flies in.”

Shamrock, a mint-green colt and one of Sapphire’s closest friends, nodded so enthusiastically that his large, black-rimmed glasses went crooked. Using her horn, Sapphire straightened them for him and then held out a large conch shell on a string. “I borrowed this from gym class. Just yell into it, and we’ll be able to hear you from across the lawn.” Shamrock slipped his horn through the string and straightened his neck so that the string fell down around his shoulders.

“Wow, cool, just like Coach Ruby!” said Firefly, a red-and-gold unicorn.

Sapphire watched Shamrock and Firefly run across the field. She still couldn’t believe they were all going to meet a real fairy tomorrow. Fairies lived throughout the five kingdoms, but as royal messengers they usually only appeared to deliver important notes or news. So you didn’t meet them unless you were someone super important. But when Sapphire's teacher, Professor Sherbet, had heard that her close friend Fairy Green was traveling through Sunshine Springs for the annual Fairy Gathering, the professor had asked if her friend could stop by to talk to the first-year students.

Ever since she was little, Sapphire had wanted to travel the five kingdoms. Growing up by the ocean, she'd seen ships travel by from all over the world. She would spend hours at her bedroom window, wondering where they were going and why. But the ships were always just out of reach, close enough to dream about but too far away for Sapphire to talk to anyone on board. So she couldn't help but feel like this meeting with Fairy Green was the start of something very big. As her good friend Twilight would say, it felt like pixies were dancing in her stomach.

It was time for stage two of the Welcome Plan. Sapphire turned to a snow-white unicorn with a red-and-white striped mane named Peppermint, and to a three-legged gray unicorn named Storm. "Okay. Is the banner ready?" Sapphire asked.

The banner certainly looked ready. Sapphire marveled at how Peppermint and Storm had managed to arrange the flowers so that they spelled out WELCOME TO UU, FAIRY GREEN! They used bright flowers for the letters and green plants for the background. Sapphire noticed that all the flowers had the same shimmer. Curious, she leaned in closer.

"I used my ability with weather to make it shine like that," Storm said proudly. "I protected the morning dew so it wouldn't dry up with the sun."

"Great work, Storm," Sapphire said with a nod of approval.

Peppermint scoffed and flipped her mane. "Well, I used my weaving ability to knit the flowers all together. We wouldn't even have a banner without me," she whined.

"Oh, it's really glitter-tastic! You guys make a fantastic team!" Comet assured her. Sapphire nudged her rose-colored friend with her flank. Comet was always so positive and encouraging. She always made everyone feel like they were part of things, like they belonged. Sapphire loved that about Comet.

"It's absolutely perfect," Sapphire agreed.

Peppermint and Storm grinned and tapped their horns together in a high-U.

"Okay, Comet," Sapphire said. "You're up next!"

Comet had woven fairy's thread through her mane, and it glittered in the bright afternoon sun. But despite all the sparkle, Comet suddenly seemed rather dull. Her eyebrows were scrunched and her mouth twisted to the side. It was a look that was certainly unusual for cheerful Comet.

"What's wrong?" Sapphire asked, her own eyebrows arching with concern.

Comet hoofed the grass beneath her. "It's just, well, I'm nervous about my part. I'm sure I can fly up to the top of the trees, no problem, and I bet I can manage to tie the ropes to the trees. Just . . . what if I can't get back down again?"

Comet had the gift of flight, but she was still learning and had a hard time with her landings. She almost never made it back down without a teacher to help. But they had all agreed to enact the Welcome Plan on their own, no grown-ups allowed.

Sapphire smiled at her sparkly friend. She knew just what to do.

"Peppermint!" Sapphire called—perhaps a little too loudly. Peppermint was right next to her, after all. "Could you weave some ivy around Comet?"

"Um, totes. That's so easy," Peppermint said with her signature mane flip. The red-and-white strands of her mane twisted and twirled together like a bunch of little candy canes. Sapphire couldn't help but admire it.

"Great," Sapphire said. "How about you wrap ivy around Comet's waist, and leave a lot of extra so I can hold one end while Comet flies up to the trees. Then, Comet, when you're ready, we'll just pull you back down again!"

A huge smile with bright pink dimples immediately replaced Comet's frown. "Let's do this!" she cheered.